THE BOAT DETECTIVE

THE BOAT DETECTIVE

RONALD HIGGINS

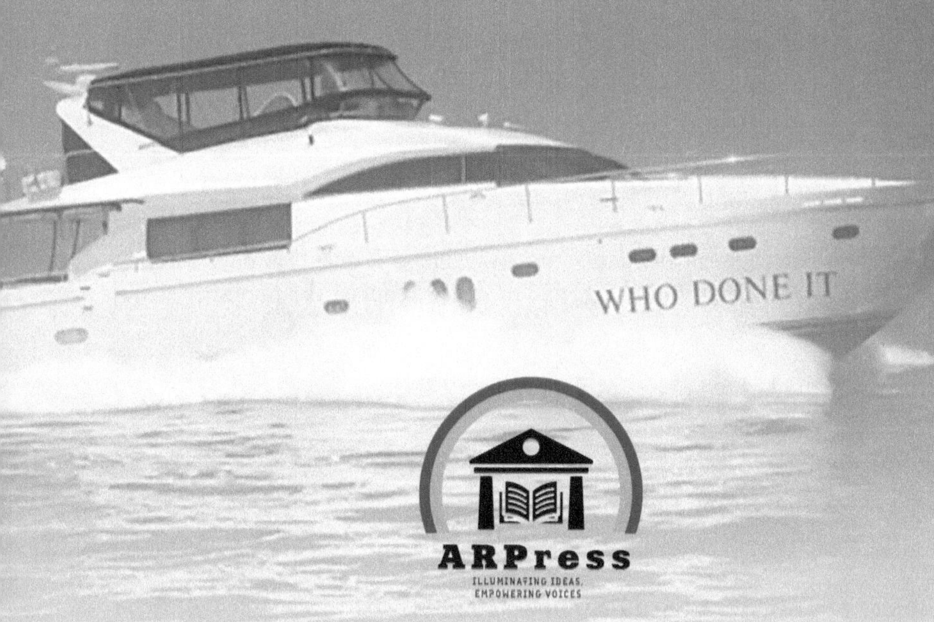

ARPress LLC
45 Dan Road Suite 5
Canton MA 02021
Hotline: 1(888) 821-0229
Fax: 1(508) 545-7580

Ordering Information:

Quantity sales. Special discounts are available on quantity purchases by corporations, associations, and others. For details, contact the publisher at the address above.

Printed in the United States of America.

ISBN-13:   Softcover   979-8-89330-395-7
           Hardcover   979-8-89330-397-1
           eBook   979-8-89330-396-4

Library of Congress Control Number: 2024901164

This is dedicated to my friend and Brother-In-Law, William Hamill, who helped me buy my first boat. Also, to my best Godson, William Hamill (Oh yes, and Only Godson)

TABLE OF CONTENTS

CHAPTER ONE

My name is Colton James, and I have a story to tell. After I opened a Detective Agency in Los Angeles, it's about my life. I worked on the NYPD for five years before my folks told me they would put money into a trust fund. When I got tired of working for the NYPD, I moved out to California, and I applied for a Private Investigation License; when I got the License, I opened my office and went into business for myself. Ever since I can remember, I always liked mystery stories about private eyes.

Anyhow with the trust fund, my parents left me. I know they were not the best jobs globally, but they always held my interest.

I opened an agency and bought a boat to live on down at Marina Del Rey. The ship is a Grand Banks, and it is forty-two-foot long. It has a couple of diesel engines, and it runs great. I called it 'The Who Done it.'

"Everything started after I moved on the boat in Marina Del Rey. It was one of those beautiful summer days that California is famous for having. I have had the yacht now for about a year. The business was okay, nothing spectacular, but it was a living. I had gone out on the boat for the day with friends and was heading back in.

My boat slowly eased into the slip with some help from the current and starboard engine power. The late afternoon sunset on the ocean is becoming another beautiful sunset in Southern California.

My friends and I took a trip down to Dana Point and back twelve hours. It was a long trip, but it was worth it. It was a pleasure to pilot my own Grand Banks up and down the coast. I had wanted one for years, so I finally decided to buy one.

Anyway, as I said we had been out all day, and now we were ready for some dinner. My girlfriend and I, along with another couple, hadn't decided where to go yet, but we were working on it while walking to the parking lot. We all agreed to go to Hooters in Santa Monica, right near the pier. I was starving. I felt like I could eat a horse. Unfortunately, they didn't have a horse. They only served chicken, but the servers were great-looking.

We all feasted on the various chicken delights on the menu. Afterward, I was ready to stop for the day. Jack and his wife Lori had gone home, and my girlfriend, Linda, and I headed back to the boat.

Jack and I met when I first arrived here from New York, or point of fact, Staten Island. After leaving the NYPD with my trust fund, I had come out here to get in the movies. Well, it didn't happen. So,

I went into the P.I business. Jack and I didn't know that we were from the same place back in New York. We had met by the pool in a North Hollywood apartment complex shortly after I arrived. Jack and I were both out by the pool, getting sun rays. We started talking and found out that we both moved out here from Staten Island at various times. Jack arrived here about three months before me. We even found out that we knew the same girl back home. Her name was Wendy, but that's another story for another day. I'm getting off the track. The first three months that Jack and I met, neither knew anything about Hollywood. We started going out to the tourist traps that were around. There was Disneyland and Universal Studios, and we can't forget the areas around Los Angeles where the Movie stars lived. There was a lot to see, that's for sure.

Anyway, I talked about that fateful day down in the Marina when Jack and Lori returned home, and Linda and I headed toward the Marina and 'The Who Done It.'

Linda and I had been going out for about five months. I met her at Venice beach. I felt a little uncomfortable going out with her considering she was so much younger than me, but she was a beauty, and up until now, that's about all I was looking forward to dating. Since moving on the boat, I had no chance to be lonely. As soon as the women find out you have a boat, they want you or want what you have. I must admit it got old after a while. Lately, I thought it was time to start looking for a long-term relationship; after all, I wasn't getting any younger. Anyway, Linda and I headed back to the boat. When we got there, I wanted to sit topside for a while and drink coffee. It was a beautiful clear night. I love looking at the evening sky with all the stars. The moon was exceptionally bright tonight; it was three-quarters full and beautiful. Linda said she was tired and wanted to go to bed. I told her I would join her in a couple of minutes.

I sat there drinking my coffee and smoking my pipe while looking across the Marina to the other side. The water was like glass, and you could see the lights from the buildings on the other side reflecting off the water.

Just then, I heard a feminine voice saying, "Good Evening."

I knew it wasn't Linda; she was below. I turned and looked on the dock, and in the moonlight was a woman with a small dog on a leash looking at me. She was standing under one of the streetlights that ran along the dock.

"Good evening. How are you?" I said.

"Just fine, I'm just taking my dog Fluffy for a walk. That's a nice boat you have."

"Thanks."

"I like her name. She must have cost a lot of money."

"You might say that, but that's okay. I can afford it."

"So, you have money, huh?" That question usually comes out at the beginning of the conversation when they see you live on a boat.

"Well, I'm all right. I don't think I'll starve. You're out late, aren't you?"

"I always take Fluffy for a walk this time of the night. It's peaceful and quiet."

I got up and walked over to the rail; I wanted to get a better look at this heavenly voice. I could see the woman was wearing red shorts and a tank top. She had long black hair hanging down over each shoulder. "What is your name?"

"Gloria, Gloria White, what's yours?"

"My friends call me Colton."

"Colton, I like that. Well, Colton, maybe I'll see you again sometime; got to go."

"Yeah, sure, see you around like an apple or orange."

I watched her walk away; the little dog was white with its tail curled in the air. I laughed as a funny thought crossed my mind. As they walked down the pier, Gloria's backside wiggled in time with the dog's butt. It struck me strange; anyway, I finished my coffee and called it a night.

The following day, I awoke at about eight a.m. I could never sleep late, even when I was a kid; I was always the first one up in the morning. I don't know. Maybe it was something in my genes. Who knows? Anyway, I got up and went to the galley, and I saw a note from Linda saying that she was up at seven and didn't want to wake me, so she took the bike and peddled over to Venice Beach, which's not too far from the Marina. In the note, she stated she would have breakfast with friends and would be back later, so much for breakfast together. I had gotten dressed and went topside. I figured I would go to the Outrigger for breakfast. I headed down the ramp. I almost ran into Gloria. She was jogging. She had on sweatpants and a yellow top with flowers on it. I knew it was Gloria because of how her hair had been flowing from side to side; also, the attractive face was a revelation.

"Good morning, Gloria."

She sidestepped me and just managed to keep me from having an early morning collision.

She smiled and said, "Well, hello, Colton. How are you this fine morning?"

She stopped for a moment, and I got a much better look at her. Last night in the moonlight, she looked younger. Now I could see her in the light of day, and she looked closer to my age. Don't get me wrong; I didn't mean she looked old; she just seemed more mature. Closer to my age than I thought last night. I liked the look.

"I noticed that fluffy wasn't running with you. Did you leave the dog home for the run?"

"Yes, I did; he is too little to keep up."

"Say I'm on my way over to the Outrigger for breakfast care to join me?"

She looked at me for a moment then said, "Sure, why not? Thanks for asking. You will have to excuse me; I'm a mess with sweat showing all over me from running and all."

"Don't worry about that; you look fine to me," I said.

She gave me one of those approving smiles, and we headed to my car.

When we climbed into my car, Gloria looked at me and said,

"Nice car."

"Yeah, well, the boat and this car were the only things I wanted to buy, so when the chance came. I bought them both."

"Good taste, blue Mercedes Benz Convertible."

"Thanks, I've always wanted one, and now, well, I got it."

I drove over to the restaurant, we didn't talk much, but I could tell that Gloria enjoyed the ride.

When we got to the restaurant, Gloria asked me, "Do you come here very often?"

I laughed and said, "That's original."

She looked at me a little strange and then caught on and smiled, then said, "Oh no, that wasn't a line, I meant it."

"I know you did. I was kidding you." We both laughed, and I continued, "I like their breakfast; I usually have steak and eggs."

She smiled, and we went inside. The server greeted us at the door.

"Morning Colton, what's on for today?

She sat us where we had a magnificent view of the Marina. I told Gloria that I usually sit when I come for breakfast. Just then, Jackie brought the menus, and I spoke, "Morning, Jackie, I'll have Steak and Eggs with Rye toast and coffee eggs over medium." I looked at Gloria.

She smiled and said, "The usual?" Then Jackie looked at Gloria and said, "What would you like?"

"Can I look at the menu for a minute?" She said to Jackie.

Jackie said, "Sure thing, take your time; I'll be back." Handing her the menu, she turned and left.

As she walked away, I said, "Say, Jackie, aren't you a little young to be working in a place that serves alcoholic beverages?"

She just smiled and said, "Colton, you wish you were this young." Then she walked back to the counter with a smile and started getting my coffee while Gloria looked over the menu.

"I take it you have been coming in here for a while now," Gloria said with a smile.

"Oh yeah, I always kid her about looking so young; it's a running joke. I've been coming in here now. Oh, I guess about two or three years now."

"That's funny, I've never seen you here, and I've been coming here for about a year myself."

"Well, I only come in for breakfast; maybe that's why."

"Yep, that must be it. I don't come in here for breakfast. Besides, I don't eat breakfast."

"Oh, what made you have breakfast today?"

"Well, to tell you the truth, I was curious about you, and when you asked me to breakfast, I figured this would give me a good chance to satisfy my curiosity."

"And have you?"

She smiled and said, "Not yet, but I'm working on it."

Just then, Jackie came back with my coffee. She looked at Gloria, saying, "Well, have you made up your mind yet?"

"Yes, I'll just have coffee and one of those coffee rings over there." She said, pointing to the basket filled with bakery items behind the counter.

When Jackie walked away, I said to Gloria, "So tell me about yourself. What kind of work do you do?"

"I'm an accountant. I work for a company over on Lincoln Blvd."

"Oh, do you own a boat?"

"Oh, goodness, no, I live in one of those condos next to the Marina. I rent. I go jogging every chance I get, and I like to look at the boats while running. So, what about you, Colton? What do you do to make all that money?"

"Are you sure you want to hear this?"

"Sure, why wouldn't I want to hear it?"

"Well, there isn't much to it. It's boring, all right, the long and short of it. Before working after college, I spent six years in the Navy as a Seal. I worked in New York City as a police officer for five years when I got out. I wanted to open my own private investigation business. My parents left me a trust fund, and I finally decided to use it. So, I moved out here about ten years ago, and at first, I thought about being in the movies, you know, as an actor, but that didn't work, so I got my Private Investigators license and started taking cases. I don't work full time, just whenever I want to. It breaks up the monotony, you know. That's it."

I could tell by the look on her face she didn't believe me.

"You got to be kidding me."

"No, that is the long and short of it."

"What kind of work did you do before you bought the boat?"

"I told you I worked at the NYPD as a police officer. I seem to have a knack for solving other people's problems. I liked the challenge. So, tell me a little something about yourself, Gloria. Are You Married?" I said.

"No, I'm widowed; my husband was one of the Passengers on Flight 93 a couple of years back. You know the flight that crashed in Pennsylvania on nine eleven. We were living in Reading, Pennsylvania, at the time."

Now I was sorry, I asked. "I'm sorry, how long had you been married?" I didn't know what to say.

"Well, we were married for three years, no children. He had a worthless younger brother; I only met him once. He was working for an investment firm. His name was Charles, Charles Cambell."

"What did Charles do? I mean, did he have a good relationship with your husband? My husband loved George, but he always bailed him out of trouble. My husband was in the process of trying to get George out of the gang in Philly. Anyway, my husband, Charles, was on his way to Washington, DC, for a business meeting when it happened. Charles, my husband, had a gambling problem too, so I had to pay off what he owed after he passed. After that, I didn't have too much money left, so I moved out to California and got an excellent job at this Accounting Company. I just had to get away."

I wanted to change the subject, so I said, "How do you like it out here now that you have been here for a while?"

She smiled and said, "I love the weather and the beaches, and the coastline is breathtaking."

"You should see it from the Ocean side," I said.

"I'd love to, but wouldn't your friend object?"

Oops, she knows about Linda. I wasn't sure what to say about that.

"Well, we will just have to play it by ear."

Gloria looked at me with a strange look and said hesitantly, "Okay."

Just then, Jackie brought us our breakfast; boy, oh boy, was I glad. There wasn't any talking while we ate. I love their steak and eggs, but I was delighted the talking had ended after that last conversation.

Gloria just finished her coffee and coffee ring and said, "Well, it's time for me to do some more jogging."

"Jogging, you are going to run home?"

"Sure, I do it all the time; it's not far. Besides, I have to run off this coffee ring."

"Will I see you again?" I said.

"I think so; what do you think?"

"I sure hope so," I said with a smile.

Gloria smiled, got up, and left. I sat there for a minute, wondering what had just happened. I was a little confused, but

I started thinking about Linda. We hadn't been getting along lately; after all, she was twenty, and I'm thirty-eight. That doesn't make the best of relationships. I mean, the sex was great, but it was after that that didn't exactly fit. We didn't have much in common. I started thinking that it sounded like I was trying to talk myself out of this relationship, to start something up with Gloria; after all, Gloria is a little older, and we probably have more in common. Just then, the servers came up to the table and spoke.

"Your friend is nice, I approve."

I laughed and said, "Well, I'm glad you do, MOM!"

"No Problem, SON...." She turned and left with a smile.

I went back to my train of thought. I knew Linda and I were coming close to the end of our relationship, and all I wanted to do was figure a way to break up without hurting Linda's feelings. Then I thought I must be crazy; I don't even know if Gloria likes me. I don't even know if Gloria would go out with me. Oh well, I'll think about it later.

Later that afternoon, while sitting topside and listening to my Kenny G CDs, Linda came up from the galley. "Say, Colton, can we talk?"

"Sure, what's up?"

"Well, I'm not sure how to say this."

I didn't like the sound of that. Whenever someone starts with, I'm not sure how to say this, you know something terrible will follow. I'm not one to evade an issue, so I said, "Come on over here and sit. Let's talk about what's bothering you."

Linda sat next to me and began, "Well, you know I enjoy being with you, and I like all the things you can give me, but I have to be honest."

Now I was curious to hear what she had to say. "Go on."

"Well, I'm just going to say it, I met someone else, and I don't want to see you anymore."

She sat there looking at me, waiting to see what I was going to say. Inside I was glad she said it because it gave me the way out of this relationship I was trying to find. At the same time, I didn't want to seem very happy in front of her, so I just said, "Oh, I see. Was it something I said?"

"Oh no, that's not it; it's just that I think I'm a little too young for you, and I think you should find someone more your age."

I couldn't believe what I was hearing. It couldn't have worked any better if I had written this as a story myself. I continued, "I see; you are a little young for me, but it was fun. Wasn't it?"

"Yes, it was, but I think it's time for me to move on."

"So, tell me, anyone I know? I mean, the gentleman you want to go out with?"

"Yes, it's Ted, you know Ted Miles."

"You mean, THE Ted Miles, the same Ted Miles whose father owns all those Real Estate Businesses and lives on that big sailboat over there on the other side of the Marina?"

"Yes, he is more my age."

I looked at her with a smile on my face and said, "Not to mention all that money he has."

"Well, yes, there is that too. A girl like me should look out for her future. Are you upset?"

"Hey, you gotta do what you gotta do." I didn't want to tell her I was glad it happened. It might hurt her feelings.

"I'll be moving my stuff out today. Ted is going to help."

"Not wasting any time, are you?"

"Well, you're here today, and Ted said he would help if I moved in now, so I thought it would be an enjoyable time to go ahead and move."

So, I said, "Well, I'm going to take in a movie this afternoon, so just leave the key on the galley countertop when you leave."

"Okay, Colton, if that's the way you want it." She had a disappointing look on her face when she spoke.

"Honestly, there is nothing wrong, I understand. I don't want to be around when Ted gets here. You've heard me talk about him, and you know how I feel. I wish you the best."

I leaned over and gave her a sweet, affectionate kiss, and said goodbye. I was happy that it turned out this way. I hated goodbyes and didn't want to be around. That's the truth of the matter.

I left and went to an afternoon movie. I don't remember what I saw. All I know is that I fell asleep and suddenly the lights came on, and the show was over. I looked at my watch, and it was about four-thirty in the afternoon. I decided to go ahead and get something to eat. I went down to the Chart House. A couple of years back, I had a smaller boat and worked for someone else. The prices were much lower than they are now. Now everything is Ah La Carte, that's where everything gets Individualized, and everything you order is separate, so instead of just buying a steak and baked potato, for example. You had to say the steak and the baked potato as side dishes. So, you paid two different prices, one for the steak and one for two side dishes, Crazy world. I finished eating at about six in the evening. I figured Linda was off the boat by now, so I headed home. It had been a long day. I didn't realize it until I climbed on board and went to the galley to fix coffee. Afterward, I went topside and smoked my pipe, drank my coffee, and just relaxed. That's one of the things I liked about having all this money. I could relax and not think about going to work the next day or what I'm going to wear or worry about having a new client bring some money in instead. I could sit on the deck and look up at the stars and let my mind wander back over the years. I didn't have to think ahead about what I would do tomorrow. It was a nice feeling. While I was doing all this heavy thinking, I heard a voice in the background. I looked over at the dock and saw Gloria. She had her dog and was taking him for a walk.

"Hi, good evening. How are you doing this evening?" I said.

"Fine, and what about yourself? How's your evening going?"

I thought for a moment and wasn't going to say anything about my roommate moving out, then I thought she would find out anyway, so why not now.

"Well, as of a few hours ago, I'm a free man sort of speak. Linda moved out."

"Oh, I'm sorry to hear that. I hope I wasn't the cause."

"No, no, that's not it, it was due; it wouldn't have worked anyway, what with our age difference and all."

"Well, anyway, I think it's her loss." She smiled when she said that. It made me feel warm and fuzzy all over.

"Would you like to come on board for some coffee?"

"No, thank you, not tonight. I must be at work early in the morning. I will try to finish everything at work in the morning, take the rest of the day off, and prepare for a long holiday weekend. I was just out walking Fluffy; then I'm headed home."

"Okay, maybe another time."

"Sounds like a plan."

I watched as she disappeared into the darkness down the pier. My mind went back to the things that happened today. It turned out to be a good day. I was happy and relieved everything turned out. It was getting late and time for me to go to bed.

I didn't realize how tired I was until I awoke the next day and discovered that it was ten in the morning. I don't usually sleep that late. Well, it was too late to go to breakfast, so I decided to skip it and catch something later. I went for a morning walk, and while I was out walking, I met Jeff Stone. Jeff is our Harbor Master for the Marina.

"Say, Jeff, how's it going?"

"Not bad, Colton; what trouble are you trying to get into this morning."

"Ha, no trouble, just going for a walk gotta keep 'in shape,' you know."

"Isn't that the truth? Gotta run, catch you later."

I watched Jeff get back on the harbor boat and head out across the Marina to his office on the other side. I'm not sure, but I think he's about fifty-one or so. I know he's retired from the Navy; I'm unsure of his rank when he left. Jeff is a helpful sort of person.

I looked at Ed McMann's boat and continued my walk. I passed his boat and couldn't help but think it was a pretty boat; he talked to this young blond-haired person on board; what else. I'll tell you these Celebes have it made. The only thing I wouldn't like about it is that you don't have any privacy. I guess when you're that famous, you should take the good with the bad. It looked like it was going to be another sweltering day. It was now about eleven-thirty. I thought maybe I'd take the boat out today and stay out for the day. I'll go down to Newport Beach or over to Catalina.

When I got back from my morning walk, I saw Gloria standing at the ramp to my boat. She was looking even better than the last time I saw her. Her long black hair was in a ponytail. I walked up to her and said with a big smile on my face. "Well, nice to see you. Did you finish everything at work like you wanted to?"

"Funny, you should ask. I got to work early this morning and finished everything that had to be done, so the boss let me have the rest of the day off. I came by to take you up on your offer for a ride and a look at the California coastline from the ocean side. I mean, since this is Friday and all, and it looks like it will be a nice weekend."

"As you said before, sounds like a plan. Come on aboard, and we'll cast off in about fifteen minutes. Where is Fluffy?"

Gloria replied, "Oh, my neighbor is watching him for the day."

I smiled and said, "Oh, good. Just let me change into something a little more workable. Help yourself to coffee in the galley. It's fresh. I'm going to change and then join you for some myself."

"Great. Think, I will."

I went to the aft stateroom to change. I couldn't believe Gloria was waiting for me at the dock. That was a pleasant surprise. It looks like it is going to be a beautiful day.

After I changed, I went topside, and Gloria was sitting drinking her coffee. "So, tell me, how much do you know about boats?" I said with a smile.

"Well, I know that the left side is called port and right-side starboard, and I know the bow is the front of the boat and stern is the rear of the boat. That about covers my knowledge of boats."

"That's a good start; that's more than I knew when I took my first ride. Okay, are you ready to cast off the lines?"

"Sure, what do you want me to do, Captain?" She said with a smile and a salute.

Colton smiled and said, "Well, you go on the dock down there and take in the stern line and the bowline. In other words, you take the two lines off of their cleats and bring them on board. I will go down and check the engines and make sure everything is ship-shape and go up to the bridge and start engines."

"Okay, that sounds good to me."

After I got back from the engine room, I watched her as she stepped off the boat onto the dock. I went up on the bridge, and I put the engine in neutral and closed the throttle all the way. I turned the key passed on to both and heard the engines turn over. I love the sound of the machines when they first startup. Gloria was down on the main deck with a thumbs-up signal to say; we're ready down here. I stared at her for a moment. The lines were on board, and Gloria stood aft and looked great, with the bright sun shining on her. She was wearing a navy-blue top and a pair of white Jeans with sunglasses. The jeans were an excellent fit. They showed every curve of her body. I put the engines in reverse and slowly backed away from the dock. I put the engines forward and gave it a little throttle when I was far enough away from the pier. I turned toward the port, and we were off. The speed is five knots while you are in the Harbor, so I set it at five knots and watched as the boat headed for the open sea. You don't make waves that are rough on other smaller ships and the floating docks. This time in the morning, the ships were already gone. The next departure from the Harbor would be much later today. It didn't take Gloria long to get by me on the bridge, and we were off for an adventure.

"Oh, Colton, it's beautiful today."

"I ordered it special, glad you like it." Gloria squeezed my arm and looked up at me with the most beautiful smile I had ever seen.

As we approached the end of the Harbor, where it opened to the sea, I took the south exit out, and after clearing the Harbor, I increased the speed to eleven knots and headed for Catalina. It was a beautiful sunny day, so I didn't have trouble seeing the island. I headed for the north end. There are two harbors on this side of Catalina. The most popular one was Avalon, and the Northern port was known as two-ports. I thought the northern end of the sanctuary was smaller and more romantic. I wanted to get to know Gloria, and this is as good a way as any to start. There is a restaurant at Isthmus that has tasty food. I figured we could go there for a late lunch. I had a couple of steaks and wine if she just wanted to eat on board.

"Well, Gloria, are you ready to take the helm?"

Gloria looked at me with a startled look and said, "Are you serious."

"Sure, why not? It's easy. Just like driving a car, only you're on the water. See that island over there? All you have to do is point the bow toward the northern end of the island."

"Which end is north?"

I laughed and said, "As you look at it, it is the right side of the island."

"Don't laugh at me." She said as she smiled.

I just patted her on the back and said, "Well, now that you have the helm, I'm going just to sit over here and relax."

Now she looked a little scared, so I said, "Don't worry, you will be fine; I'll be right over here if you need me. You'll love it. I promise you."

"You are pretty sure of yourself, aren't you?"

"Yep, all my friends said the same thing when they took the helm for the first time. After they had it for about fifteen minutes or, so I couldn't get them away from the wheel, you'll see."

Gloria looked as though she had been piloting a boat all her life. I knew she wouldn't have a problem. There weren't any boats around that she could hit, and we were far enough from shore that she wouldn't run into any rocks.

"Well, how are you doing?"

Gloria turned and looked at me with a smile on her face that said, okay, so it's not that hard. Then she told me, "Say this is a lot of fun. I could get used to this."

"Told you, now it will take us about two hours to get to Catalina, so just relax and enjoy the trip."

"Oh, Colton, you were right. It's beautiful out here. I never knew it could be so beautiful, but it is; look at that Coastline."

Gloria would never forget the feeling of looking at that shoreline and how she felt when she did. I moved up and sat down next to her, and we just enjoyed each other's company for the next two hours.

"So, tell me, Colton, since your retirement, what do you do for fun?"

"Just what we're doing, you know, I was thinking the other day. I don't miss work at all. I wake up every morning and then decide what I want to do. Sometimes something pops into my head the night before, and then when I wake up in the morning, I've changed my mind, and I want to do something else."

"It must be nice not to have to worry about where your next dollar comes from; besides your boat, what other hobbies do you have?"

"Well, I like to go to movies and take the

car on trips to places I haven't been to. I also like to play golf. Oh yes, I also have a Harley Trike. You know, a three-wheel motorcycle-only, it has two wheels in back and one in the front."

Gloria had this puzzled look on her face, "Harley? That sounds like fun; maybe we can take a ride on that too."

I couldn't help it; I just laughed and told her. "Sounds like a plan. Enough about me, tell me about you. What do you do these days for fun?"

You saw it when you met me. I love to run; I get great satisfaction from running. It's like any problem or situation I might have on my mind floats away when I'm running."

"That's the same way I feel about boating. When I'm out on the boat, the sea air makes everything else seem less important."

"That's it exactly. Of course, I also have Fluffy; he is an excellent company. Colton, one thing I'm finding out about boating. It seems like we are going faster than we are."

"How fast do you think you're going right now? Don't look."

"I don't know, maybe thirty-five or forty miles an hour."

I started to laugh, "You are laughing at me again. Stop that."

"I'm sorry, I didn't mean to laugh. We are only going about ten miles or so an hour."

She looked at me in amazement, "You're kidding!"

"Nope, you are right about the fact that you feel like you are going faster than you are."

I pushed the throttle forward and said, "Let's go faster. I want to get to Catalina before noon."

"Look in the water by the bow of the boat. There are dolphins following us on each side of the boat. They do that all the time."

"Wow, look at the dolphins, aren't they beautiful. Will they stay there all day?"

"Well, they will stay there until they get tired or bored, then they will leave."

"They swim so beautifully."

"They should; they went to school for it at an early age."

For a minute straight-faced, Gloria looked at me, then slowly, a smile came through and lit up her whole face, then she said straight-faced, "No kidding."

We both laughed.

"So, tell me, Colton, how long have you been going over to Catalina?"

"Well, I've only had this boat going on two years, and in that time, I guess I've been over to Catalina about a dozen times or so. Before that, I lived on the land for nine years and hated it."

"What was so bad about it?"

"Well, I guess I was tired of solving other people's problems and getting hit over the head a lot."

"Yeah, here you are today with all the money you will ever need. Are you happy?"

"Yep, that's the truth.

 I got enough to do me for a while."

"I'll bet you do."

"I think it's a little more now, what with my investments and all."

"You said this time. Have you lived on a boat before?"

"Yes, I had another boat that was smaller than this one. It was easier to keep clean. My job was to get people to look at this boat club down in Newport Beach. While waiting for my Private Detective license to get processed, I was a salesperson. Back in 1991, I won a free membership at a Yacht Club in Newport Beach. It was one of those promotional things they do to get you to join the boat club. When I got to the Yacht Club, I didn't know much about boats. I started hanging out with this guy who captured a cruise boat for the club. He took people out in one of the club's boats to entice people to buy their boats and use their club as their home port. He was about ten years younger than me, but we got along pretty well. He captained a forty-two-footer that belonged to the club. The boat would take people on a tour of Newport Beach Harbor every Saturday and Sunday, and then he tries to get them to join the club. I would come down and go out with him, and he would show me the ropes. When the tour was over, he would teach me how to dock that baby at the end of the day. I liked it and decided that I wanted a boat of my own. Of course, I couldn't afford a big boat like that, so I bought a little twenty-eight-foot Bayliner single-engine. It slept five and cruised at about twenty-one knots. I lived on it for about three years then decided that it wasn't large enough, but I still couldn't afford another boat, so I bought a condominium in Azusa. Then when my trust fund kicked in, I bought this one. Say I'm talking too much."

"No, I enjoyed hearing about it."

"Well, I must say that's very nice of you, so tell me something about yourself."

"Where shall I start? I told you about my husband Charles and me. I'm Gloria from Reading, Pennsylvania."

I enjoyed my time with Gloria so much that I suddenly realized we were only about a mile from the Catalina shores. So, I told Gloria to let me take the wheel.

As we got closer to the island's northern part, they called port Isthmus. I called the Harbor Master on the radio and asked him which Anchorage he wanted us to use. After finding it, I stopped the engines and coasted toward the pull pole. I told Gloria that she could pull the rod out of the water, and there would be an anchor line on the end of it, and all she had to do was attach it to the cleat on the boat's port bow side. She did an excellent job.

After securing the stern line, I called the taxi patrol and requested that they pick us up on the boat's starboard side in about ten minutes. I looked at my watch; it was one forty-five. We made a pretty good time coming over. After about ten minutes, the taxi pulled alongside the boat. Gloria and I climbed aboard, and the taxi headed to shore. When we got ashore, we walked along the beach for a while. It was a beautiful day, and Gloria made the day seem even more beautiful than it was if that's possible.

"Colton, this is so nice and beautiful. It is so peaceful over here, almost as if we are a million miles from the Mainland."

"That's one of the things I like about being able to come over here anytime I want. I feel like I could be anywhere in the world I want to be. You should see it at night. Wait until the stars come out tonight."

We walked along the beach for a while. Gloria found seashells in the sand. She wanted to keep them as a memento of our trip to Catalina.

"Well, Gloria, are you hungry yet?"

"Are you kidding? This sea air makes you hungry in a hurry. I'm ready whenever you are. Where do we go to eat around here?"

"Well, Miss White, I just happen to know a place close by." I finished the sentence, and Gloria turned, and we were right in front of the restaurant.

Gloria turned back to me with a big smile on her face and said, "

Wise guy, huh." She gave me an affectionate punch in the stomach.

We proceeded to the restaurant. Inside we met up with Jim.

"Say, Jim, I'd like you to meet a friend of mine. Gloria White Gloria, Jim, the best cook on the island, also owns this establishment. Jim, how about the best booth in the House? We'll be having a late lunch."

Jim smiled, "Sure thing, Mr. James, for you nothing but the best."

I thought this was, without a doubt, one of the most delightful days I've had in a long time. The booth was just right. It faced the seaside of the island. We could see my boat from where we sat. A beautiful woman is sitting across from me. After Jim left to get our drinks, I noticed Gloria's staring. "What's wrong?"

"Nothing, I was just thinking, you have it made, don't you?"

"Oh, I don't know. I guess it's better than some but not as good as others. I'm happy with where I am right now in my life. What about you?"

"Well, I guess I'm where I want to be now. Although there is still more, I want to do before my life finishes."

"Like what?"

"Oh, I don't know. I want to be married again and maybe have children. Two, I think a girl and a boy."

"You're young yet; I'm sure it'll happen for you."

Jim came over and asked what we wanted to eat. We told him, and he left. It was still early after eating lunch, so we took the bus ride south to Avalon. It is only about a thirty-minute trip. When we got to Avalon, I was glad it was still early. The shuttle boat hadn't arrived from Long Beach. We walked around the shops for a while. You know all those places you buy gifts that say Catalina Island on them. Then when you get home, you show them to all your friends, making them wish they had taken the trip instead of you. After an hour of walking around the shops, I was ready to call it a day. I asked Gloria if she was prepared to take the bus back to the boat.

"What's the matter? Tired?" She said with a big grin.

"Yes, as a matter of fact, I am!"

"Okay," she continued, "Let's catch the bus."

We didn't say much on the bus ride back, but I couldn't keep my eyes off Gloria. She caught me a couple of times and just smiled. We got to the dockside about five-thirty in the evening. I asked Gloria if she wanted to get something to eat, but she said no. It had been a full day for both of us. We decided to head back to Marina Del Rey. It was a great ride back.

"Doesn't the sun look beautiful?" I heard Gloria say. "You think that's beautiful? It's supposed to be a full moon tonight. Wait and see, by the time we get back to the Marina, the moon will be out, and that will be even prettier. You will be able to see the stars I was talking about; they seem to go on forever."

"It's been a wonderful day," Gloria said.

She was sitting next to me at the helm. I felt so close to her at that moment. I didn't want to go too fast and spoil it. When she turned and looked at me and smiled, I lost it. I couldn't get over how beautiful she looked in this light. I leaned over and gave her a little peck on the lips. She didn't make a move to stop me, so I figured everything was all right.

We arrived back at the Marina just as the sun was setting. It always looks pretty, but tonight it looked even more beautiful than I've seen it in a long time. We sat topside and drank coffee, and she told me about her childhood growing up in Reading. Her father was an insurance salesperson and traveled. Her mother did the raising. Before we knew it was almost eleven p.m., I walked her home, asking her if I could see her tomorrow. I was glad when she said yes. I made my way back to the boat and went to bed. I had trouble sleeping. I was thinking of Gloria and how wonderful she was. I finally closed my eyes around two-thirty.

CHAPTER THREE

I awoke and looked at the clock; it was almost eleven. I got up and called Gloria on the phone and asked if she wanted to have lunch. She said yes, and I told her I would pick her up outside her complex around noon. I hung up the phone and started dressing.

I got in front of Gloria's place around noon. I saw two dark-skinned men in suits talking to her. She looked upset, and then one of them grabbed her like they were trying to take her somewhere she didn't plan to go. I jumped out of the car and ran up to them. "Say bud, hold up there. Can't you see the little lady doesn't want to go?" I grabbed the guy holding her first and cracked him across the jaw, and he went down. I turned in time to catch the second one swinging at me. I ducked and hit him in the stomach. That usually discourages someone from trying something else. He doubled up but came right back with a left hook that left me spinning to the sidewalk. By the time I got up, the two were running down the street. I went to Gloria, who, by this time, was picking herself up. I helped her up and asked, "Are you okay? Who were they? What did they want?"

She looked like she didn't want to go into it right now and said, "It was nothing; I'm sorry you had to see it."

"No, I'm glad to have been of some help. No telling what would have happened if I weren't here."

I helped Gloria into my car, and we headed off to lunch.

When we finally got to the restaurant and sat down, Gloria still looked a little shaken up.

"Do you want to talk about it?"

She looked at me like she didn't want to, so I said, "You will feel better if you get it out of your system."

"I'm not sure who they were. Remember me telling you about Charles, which was my husband's name; anyway, he was working for a firm in Reading?"

"Yes, what does that have to do with these guys?"

"Everything, I think. I told you already, anyway, the company dealt mainly with the Middle East. You see, when my husband died, he was working for an Investment firm. He found out something about the company he wasn't supposed to know."

"Do you think it had anything to do with the hijacking of his plane?"

"I don't think so, but I don't know; my husband told me before he took that flight that if anything happened to him, I was to disappear someplace. So when the plane got hijacked, I ran as quickly as I could and settled out here and changed my name back to my maiden name, hoping I would be safe. I was up until today."

"What was your married name? Do you know what they were after?"

"My married name was Gloria Cambell. I'm not sure what they were after. When my husband got killed, I packed up, took his things, and left. I haven't looked at what he had in the boxes. I just grabbed everything I could and left."

"Maybe it was the time you looked to see if he has anything that they might want. They might come back now that they know where you live. Why don't you get fluffy and whatever personal things you need and move on board for a while? They don't know me, so they know where I live.

I could always take you and fluffy over to Catalina for a while. They won't find you there."

"I hate to put you out. Besides, what would I do? I have my job?"

"Can't you request a leave of absence only don't tell them where you are going? Just tell them it's an emergency."

Gloria thought for a moment and then said, "Yes, I suppose I could do that. Are you sure you don't mind? I hate to get you involved in this."

"I'm already involved; besides, I was getting bored with being retired. It's time I had a project to work on."

I hated to see her going through this with no help. Of course, there was that voice in my head saying, 'watch out, buddy, you might be taking on too much.' As usual, I was ignoring it. "Don't worry. Everything will be fine. Why don't you go upstairs, and you can throw things in a suitcase?

Tell your property owner you're going away for a while, but don't tell her where, and you will send her the rent when it's due. Don't forget to bring whatever your husband's things were so you could look through them later. Maybe we can figure out what they were after. Do you need me to help?"

She said, "No, that's all right, I got this. You can wait here. Okay?"

I answered, "sounds like a plan."

She came back out with a suitcase and two small boxes. It took her about half an hour or so. I helped her in the car with the stuff, and I asked, "Where is Fluffy.?"

Gloria looked at me a little uncomfortable and said, "oh, I asked my neighbor to watch her for a while until I get settled. She loves to take care of Fluffy whenever she can; Fluffy doesn't like the water."

We headed to the dock. When we got to the 'The Who Done it,' I took the boxes and suitcase, and Gloria followed me on the boat. I took everything below and put it in the other stateroom I had. I was glad I had just put clean sheets on the bed that morning. I usually change the sheets every two weeks, whether they need it or not. While she settled in, I went to the galley and fixed fresh coffee. After a while, Gloria came in. I gave her a cup. It was only about two-thirty in the afternoon. I told her we could make it over to Catalina before dark; that way, she could rest, and we wouldn't have any unwanted guests. Gloria agreed. So, while she drank the coffee and tried to relax for a couple of minutes, I went topside, took in the lines, went to the bridge, and started the engines. Minutes later, and while we were still in the Harbor heading out to Sea, Gloria joined me at the helm. She brought me coffee, and I thanked her.

She said, "No, thank you. I'm sorry to put you through all this."

"Oh, don't worry. It's my pleasure. I enjoy having you around."

She just smiled, drank her coffee, and watched as we left the Harbor and headed to Catalina. It was one of those beautiful summer afternoons. The sky was blue, and it reflected on the water. I put her at twelve knots and headed for Isthmus. We would be there before dark.

CHAPTER FOUR

I tied up at the mooring and went down into the Salon. It was about four-thirty. Gloria was asleep on the sofa. I didn't want to disturb her, so I went into the stateroom where she would be staying and put her suitcase on the bed and her husband's boxes of personal things on the floor next to the wall.

When I got back to the Salon, Gloria was sitting on the sofa. She was awake now, looking at me. She was calm enough to talk about her situation. We went and sat on the aft deck, and I fixed us fresh coffee.

She started, "I had only been his wife for about a year and a half when he got this job. The name of the place was 'Moore for Less.' The owner of the company was Albert Moore. He was in the Investment aspect of the business. My husband Charles had only been with the company for less than a year. They dealt with different clothing styles all over the world. I'm not sure how it worked. I never could get the process of the whole thing. There was always too much to memorize anyway. Charles had no problem with it. Charles, that was my husband's name. He would come home from work and talk about the Investment business, and I had no idea what he was talking about. I mean, I'm good with American styles of clothing but not the foreign market."

"Well, lady, we're in the same boat there. I wouldn't have any idea what he was talking about either. All I know about is the American dollar. Did you know those two guys that were trying to rough you up this morning?"

"No, but you know, one of them did look familiar. The taller one, I've seen that man somewhere. I used to go to Charles's office and sometimes bring him lunch or go out. I saw him there at the office. Now that I think about it, he was there. It was about two weeks before Charles."

I could see her eyes start to water as she spoke.

"You don't have to talk about it now if you don't want to. I mean, there is always tomorrow after you get some rest."

"No, that's okay. I want to." She continued, "He came to visit Charles's boss, Mr. Osama, about something to do with a transaction with the company and somebody in the middle-east. He mentioned his name while I was there. I can't remember it right now."

I didn't think tonight was an enjoyable time to talk about it. It could wait until tomorrow. Besides, Gloria needed a good night's sleep, and this salt air would ensure that.

"Listen, Gloria, why don't you get some shut-eye, and we can talk some more over a nice hot breakfast in the morning. How's that sound?"

"Yeah, maybe you're right. I am tired of boat rides. Do they always make you sleepy, or is it just me?"

"Trust me; you will sleep well tonight. I made your bed in the forward cabin right down those stairs." He said, now pointing to the stairs to his left.

Gloria got up and headed down the stairs. Halfway down, she stopped and turned and said, "Colton, thanks for being here for me. I appreciate it." She turned and continued down the stairs. I heard her door shut.

I sat topside for a bit longer, drinking my coffee and going over in my mind what she had just told me. I wanted to help her.

My vacation was too long; it was time to get back to work. I will have to use my contacts and see if they can help. I'll make calls tomorrow. Cell phones are great on boats. First, I want to give her a couple of days to relax and forget her troubles. I think the next couple of weeks will be hard for her.

I'll try calling Joe Williamson to see if he is still working at the downtown marketing center. He'll help. I had just moved out here and bought this boat. He used to work in New York when I was still a cop, and he worked downtown in the Market District. Besides, he owes me a favor when I helped him with that incident dealing with that extraordinary man from Holland, who was in some kind of trouble. Günter Hemlock was into race horsing. He was always trying to make his bets a sure thing. Joe wanted me to track Gunter while he was in L.A. Now that was a tailing job. He took me all over downtown L.A. It was only supposed to be a couple of days, and it lasted for two weeks. Not to mention it got me beat up twice before the job had finished. I gave Joe the hospital bill. Günter wasn't very organized. He was running around, trying to make connections with a bookie. I don't think Günter was very good at his job, or he was new at it and hadn't been in L.A. too many times in the past. Come to find out later that he was a bookie from Amsterdam. He owned a small shop on the outskirts of town, and he owed money to other bookies in town and couldn't pay them.

The bookie suggested he sell his diamonds in the states to get the money to pay them off. Why he came out here to L.A. instead of New York is beyond me. He wasn't a brilliant guy. After they arrested him, the truth came to the surface. They found out that he had been doing this kind of work for a couple of years. He had a job with the syndicate, working out of Holland. I looked at my watch, and it was twelve-thirty. I got up and went downstairs to get some shut-eye. I went to my cabin, and I no sooner undressed and climbed into bed, and I was out like a light.

CHAPTER FIVE

I awoke to the smell of my favorite coffee. I knew I didn't make it. So, I dressed and headed for the galley. When I entered the galley, I saw Gloria sitting at the table drinking coffee.

"Good morning, Gloria. How are you doing this morning? Did you sleep all right on that bed?"

"Yes, that was the best sleep I've had for a while; it must have been the sea air. I made some coffee.:"

"It was probably a combination of the sea air and easy swaying of the boat in time with the current and the fact that you were tired anyway; I think that did it."

"Well, whatever it was, it worked. I feel like a million bucks." With that, she walked up to me, threw her arms around me, and kissed me. I was not expecting her to do that, and I was surprised.

She could tell by the look on my face. "Oh, I am sorry. I shouldn't have assumed that you wanted me to kiss you."

"No, no, I'm glad you did. I would have done it myself except that I was a little confused about when you would be ready for me to kiss you."

"Well, I guess that takes all the confusion out."

"Yeah, I guess it does." With that said, I moved in closer, put my arms around her, and kissed her. She kissed me back; everything just went into slow motion after that. When we finally stopped kissing, she looked at me, and I knew it wasn't going to end there. She took my hand and led me down the stairs to her room when we entered. She looked at me and said, "I want to do this, okay?"

I couldn't be more pleased. But I wasn't sure what to say to that, so I just said, "Me too."

Our bodies stood close together, feeling the electricity coming from both our inner beings. I kissed Gloria's neck as Gloria's fingers explored the back of my head and down my back. Everything floated off into another dimension in time where pleasure has its home and desire exists; this was a good thing. I knew this was where I wanted to be and who that person was, Gloria. I could tell she felt the same way.

I didn't know how long we were in her room. All I remember was the sun rose again, and out came a new day. It was bright and fresh, and Gloria was lying beside me. I watched her sleep; she looked like an angel. There is something beautiful about watching a woman sleeping. It makes you feel good to be a man knowing this woman wanted you, and at the same time, you knew she needed you. At that moment, I wanted and needed her too. She rolled over toward me and opened her eyes. Looking at me, she smiled and said, "Good morning, sweetheart."

Sweetheart, that is a word a man can't hear too much from a woman. I looked back at her and said, "Morning! It's late afternoon. Are you hungry?"

She kissed me and said, "Well, are You?"

The way she said that made me feel something I hadn't thought about for a long time, secure and all warm insides.

"I have a couple of steaks I can cook along with eggs and coffee and toast. How does that sound?"

"Perfect, while you're fixing the food, I'll take a shower and dress."

"Sounds like a plan. " I got out of bed, put on my bathrobe, and headed to the galley. I first made fresh coffee, poured a cup for myself, put the steaks on low, and went topside to look at this beautiful day. It was beautiful and quiet topside. Catalina was a sight to see this time of day.

I turned in time to see Gloria coming up topside. She was wearing a beautiful blue tank top with matching shorts. I must say I've never seen anything this beautiful.

"Good morning, Colton." She leans in and kisses me.

"Gloria, you are sure making it hard for me to think about the food I'm cooking." She backed up and twirled around, showing off her outfit and body while saying, "Am I, Gee, I'm sorry." She had the biggest smile on her face. I could tell she was enjoying her little tease.

I went down and finished making the food while Gloria went in and started going through her husband's private boxes.

After we ate, we sat topside, and Gloria talked to me about her husband.

"You know, Colton, while going through my husband's things, I recalled where I saw that man. You know, the one that was getting rough with me outside my apartment."

"Yeah, okay, so who was he?"

"Well, I saw him at my husband's office when I went there to take Charles out to lunch. It must have been oh a month or so before the 911 incident. I remember they were arguing about something, but I couldn't hear what it was. I was in the outer office, and they were in the inner office. All I know is Charles was yelling loud. When I knocked on the door, all the yelling ended, and the door opened. The man left, but not before saying, 'remember what I told you could happen.' And then he left"

"Did you hear a name?"

"No, all I remember was that Charles was so upset he didn't want to go to lunch, and he asked me to leave. He said he would meet me later at home, so I left."

"Did you see that man at all after that day?"

"No, but I think he called the house once after that."

"Why do you say that?"

"Well, one evening a couple of weeks later, we were both sitting in the reading room, that's what we called our library because we both used that room for reading, the phone rang. I picked it up as I normally did when we were home. Charles didn't like to get interrupted when reading, so I always answered the phone. The man asked for Charles, and I recognized the voice and remembered it sounded like the man in Charles's office that day. I handed the phone to Charles, and after he answered the phone and heard the man's voice, he got up and went into the other room and took the call. I didn't hear the conversation after that."

"How was Charles's demeanor after the phone call?"

"He was upset for the rest of the night. I asked him what was bothering him, but he wouldn't say.

A couple of days after that came 911. We all know what happened that day."

"Yes, our world as we know it was changed forever," Colton said.

Gloria responded with, "Well, now you know as much as I know. What's next?"

"Well, Gloria," Colton continued, "You will relax and not worry about anything; I'm going to make a few calls and see what I can find out."

CHAPTER SIX

When Colton had finished making the phone calls he wanted, he went topside to see Gloria. Colton was surprised to see Gloria had put a bathing suit on and sunbathed when he reached the top deck. Gloria was wearing a beautiful red bikini; Colton couldn't take his eyes off her. She was lying there in a deck chair. Gloria was sound asleep. When Colton approached her, she jumped up from a sound sleep with a frightened look.

"Whoa, hold up, it's only me. You're safe."

Gloria looked at Colton and put her arms around him, squeezed tight, then spoke, "Oh Colton, hold me, don't let me go. I'm scared."

"There is nothing to be afraid of, you're on my boat, and it's just the two of us; nobody else is on board. Easy now; relax." When Colton spoke, he had his hands on both of Gloria's arms and looked right at her.

Gloria realized she was having a bad dream and pulled away from Colton and said, "I'm sorry I had a bad dream. I'm all right now." While she spoke, she stood up and walked away from Colton to the other side of the boat. Colton wasn't going to push the issue. He knew she was thinking about the two men approaching her, and she was worried.

Colton spoke first, "Well, I made a few calls around town and found out that the two men that hassled you the other day are part of a syndicate that's moving in out here, from Philadelphia. It's headed up by Joey Gardeano (Joey the Rascal).

When we get back to the Mainland, I will quickly visit him and find out exactly what he wants from you. So, relax and enjoy the rest of the trip. Everything is going to be all right."

CHAPTER SEVEN

"What did you say? Joey the Rascal?" Gloria said it with fear in her voice, and Colton heard it. He turned and looked at her and said, "yes, so what."

Gloria replies, "I've heard that name." She snaps her fingers and then replies, "Yes, of course, I heard that name. Joey Gardeano was one of the leaders of the gangs where George belonged. I remember Charles telling me about him."

"Really!" Said Colton. "Do you remember the name for the Gang?" Colton was standing over Gloria and looking down, waiting for an answer. Gloria was trying to think what she heard from Charles and spoke, "yes, it was a strange phase; when I heard it, it sounded like a funny kind name for a gang. Let me see; oh yes, I remember now they called themselves the "Peace Eaters."

Colton repeats it, "The Peace Eaters." That's a funny name for a gang."

"Yes, I thought so too. Charles explained that it meant anybody that was for peace would be eaten up, and then they would spit them out."

"Well, when we get back to the Mainland. I'm going to visit Mr. Gardeano and ask him a few questions."

Gloria jumped up out of the chair, put her arms around Colton, and spoke, "oh, Colton, be careful; these are bad people to mess with it. Colton looked into Gloria's eyes and spoke, "Oh, I'm just going to ask him a couple of questions. Don't worry, honey, and I'll be fine." He looks into Gloria's eyes and thinks he wanted her that minute. He pulls her closer and kisses her. While he is kissing her, he realizes he doesn't have time for that. He had to get to the mainland and see Mr. Gardeano.

He pulls away from Gloria and speaks, "wait, honey, we don't have time for this. We got to get back to the mainland. I have a business, remember."

Gloria has a disappointed look on her face and replies, "I know Mr. Gardeano." She looks at Colton real seriously and says, "Remember what I said about being careful. He is a heavyweight."

Colton looks at Gloria, points at her, and says, "Say, honey, don't worry, I'm a pretty good heavyweight myself." Then he smiled and headed to the helm. As he grabs the wheel, he turns and says to Gloria, "Say honey let loose of the stern and bow lines for me please while I check the engines." She waves in agreement as she heads for the stern line.

Minutes later, we see the boat easing away from the buoy and toward the Mainland. Colton gives it gas, and the ship heads toward the ocean back to the Mainland.

CHAPTER EIGHT

It was early afternoon when the boat eased into the slip of the Marina. It took them about ninety minutes. That's pretty good. Gloria tied up the stern line as Colton was getting the bowline secured. They meet in the middle, and Colton speaks, "Gloria, you stay here. I'm going to meet with Mr. Gardeano. I'll only be about an hour or so. He has an office, unbelievably, in North Hollywood on Lankershim Blvd."

Gloria speaks, "Be careful, Colton; that man is sad news."

Colton jumps off the deck, waves back at Gloria, and says, "Don't worry, I will see you in a couple of hours." He says as he disappears around the corner to the parking lot.

Colton reaches North Hollywood in about forty-five minutes, which is pretty good considering the time of day; the freeway was clean. He finds a spot to park on Lankershim, and it is only two blocks from Mr. Gardeno's place.

Colton walks to the store in front of Mr. Gardeno's place. The sign on the front windows says in big blocks letters, "The Only Place in Town That Gives you An Honest Loan For Your Return."

Colon continues reading underneath it with big block letters "Proprietor- Mr. Joe Gardeno – Loan Officer.

Colton stands there looking at the sign and smiles and says to himself, 'Yeah, right. I'll bet.'

He opens the door and walks inside. The redheaded secretary looks up from her work, smiles at Colton, and says, "Yes, sir, can I help you?"

Colton answers, "Yes, in fact, you can. I'm here to see Mr. Gardeno. Can you please tell him Mr. James is here?"

The secretary reply's back, "May I know what it is about?"

"Tell Mr. Gardeno I want to talk to him about Mrs. Cambell. He'll know what I mean."

The redhead got up and walked into the other office. Meanwhile, Colton turned around to find a seat to wait. He noticed a man tall and skinny walking up to him and started speaking.

"Excuse me, sir. I couldn't help but overhear what you said to the secretary. You have a business to discuss with Mr. Gardeano about Mrs. Cambell?"

Colton says, "Yes, well, what business is that of yours?"

Then the man jumped right in with, "I'm George Cambell, her husband's brother. Where is she?"

George Cambell stood about five foot ten, not much taller. He was a slim man dressed in jeans and a plaid shirt with a vest and cowboy hat. He looked like something out of a bad Western.

Colton didn't want to get into it with Mr. Cambell. It wasn't the right time.

Colton continues, "I'm trying to find her, and I was told Mr. Gardeano might know.

George, with a big grin on his face, chimes in with, "I doubt he knows. None of us do. Where did you get that idea?"

Just then, the secretary came out of Mr. Gardeno's office and spoke.

"Mr. James, Mr. Gardeano will see you now."

Colton smiles at Cambell and says, "Excuse me."

He turns and heads over toward Mr. Gardeno's office and closes the door behind him.

Colton walks in, and Mr. Gardeano speaks first.

"Mr. James, won't you sit here."

Colton sits at the seat that Mr. Gardeano had pointed to in front of the desk.

Mr. Gardeano continues. "So, what business brings you to my office?"

Colton speaks, "we know a mutual friend Mrs. Cambell. Last week a couple of your men approached her, and I was wondering what they were looking for?"

Mr. Gardeano rocked back on his chair and smiled, then said, "What business is that of yours?

Colton continues, "Well, Mrs. Cambell is a client of mine."

That got the attention of Mr. Gardeano, and now he leans forward and puts both elbows on his desk and says, "Client, what kind of client is that? Exactly, what kind of business are you in, Mr. James?"

Colton reaches in his pocket, pulls out a business card, hands it to Mr. Gardeano, then speaks, "My name is Colton James, Private Investigator. Mrs. Cambell has hired me to investigate the Murder of her Husband."

"Mr. James, are you saying that I might have something to do with that?"

"No, sir, not at all. I just wondered why a couple of your men last week tried to persuade Ms. Cambell to go with them when she didn't want to go. I had to step in and clarify it more for them."

Mr. Gardeano shows interest now by getting up and walking around the desk to sit on the corner with his arms folded and continues speaking, "Is that so? Well, I'm sorry that happened, Mr. James. It was just a little business between Ms. Cambell and me. My men probably got a little carried away. I'll talk to them. Is there anything else I can help you with, Mr. James?"

Colton stands too and says, "No, that should do it. If you have business with her again, you will have business with me, and I promise, you won't like it." Colton turns and leaves the office. On his way out of the outer office, he waves to Mr. Cambell and walks out the door.

The traffic was heavier heading south on the 170. It took Colton longer to get back to the Marina. By the time he got back to the boat, it was dinner time. While Colton was stepping on board the ship, he could smell his favorite dinner. Gloria had fixed him Catfish dinner with some French fries topped off with a cold Pepsi. He entered the galley, greeting Gloria with, "That's just what the doctor ordered." He said to Gloria as he sat at the table looking at her; she was complete with an apron and a smile. She spoke with a curious look saying, "How did it go with Mr. Gardeano today?"

"It was interesting. I saw your Husband's brother George. He was there and asked where you were, and I told him that is what I was trying to find out."

Gloria laughed and said, "That should keep him guessing for a while."

Colton wanted to change the subject. "Enough business for today. What did you do while I was gone besides fix this beautiful meal?"

"Well, after you left, I went back to sleep for a couple of hours and went for a walk along the dock. Then came back and fixed dinner for you. After all, I do have to work for my stay on the boat."

They both smiled, and Colton continued with, "Well, maybe you also had time to make some dessert?" Gloria answered, "Oh, I have something special for later." Again, Colton smiled and said, "I can't wait."

CHAPTER NINE

Later that night, Colton and Gloria walked together on the dock, holding hands, and looking at all the boats there. Suddenly, a dark figure came up behind Colton and grabbed him by the neck. Colton flipped the man in the water with one smooth move, and the second took a swing at Colton. Colton ducked and came back with a hard right to the stomach, which doubled the other man, and he went down hard, and Colton could see that it was one of the men that tried to take Gloria away the other day. Colton kicked him in the face, and the guy was out to lunch. Colton took Gloria by the hand and said, "C'mon, run back to the boat. They ran about seventy-five feet, and Colton turned and didn't see any of the two men following, so he said, to Gloria, "Let's get on the boat and take it out of the harbor before they get a good look; at it."

Colton turned down the pier toward the boat and shouted to Gloria, "Gloria unties the bowline and jump on the boat, and I'll get the stern line." Colton, right behind her, jumped on the boat, headed for the wheelhouse, and started the engines. It was dark by then, so Colton slowly backed the boat away from the dock and led to the central part of the bay, ensuring he kept the speed within the Harbor limits. He was heading toward the opening. Gloria went up to the wheelhouse to find out what had just happened. When she got there, Colton turned the boat onto the central part of the bay and headed toward the Port's exit.

Gloria spoke first, "Colton, what just happened?"

Colton turned to Gloria and said, "Nothing we have to worry about for the moment. I will tell you those two men were the same to men that tried to carry you off the other day in front of your house."

Gloria had a surprised look on her face and said, "Colton, are you sure? What do you suppose they wanted?"

"I don't know, but I wasn't going to stick around to ask. Look, I have a friend that runs the marina up at Santa Barbara; I'm heading there now. We will be safe there for a while. Listen, Gloria; it will take us a while to get there. In the meantime, why don't you go down to the cabin and look through those things of your husband's and see if you can find anything that might give us a clue."

"Okay, you got it. I'll go down now." Gloria turned and headed down to the cabin. After Gloria leaves the helm, Colton calls his bubby and Harbor Master at Santa Barbara Harbor Jack Terrana and asks him if he could make the arrangements for this boat to a place to stay for a couple of days? Jack was glad to do it.

A couple of hours later, Colton's boat pulls into the harbor. Colton calls Jack and lets him know he is entering the port, and Jack tells him the slip number and where it is located. Colton pulls into the slip and stops all engines as the boat eases in to place at the boat slip. Colton climbs off the ship, ties the bowline to the cleat, and does the same for the stern line. Colton would check in with Jack around noon tomorrow. It was late; he went down the stairs to Gloria's cabin and checked in to see if she was okay. He sees her sleeping; he smiles and goes to his cabin and bed.

CHAPTER TEN

olton awakes to the smell of fresh coffee. He dressed and headed to the galley.

He enters the galley and sees Gloria making breakfast. He speaks, "Well, it smells great in here. Is it your perfume or the great breakfast you are preparing?"

Gloria turns with a smile on her face and says, "I'm fixing breakfast for you. Also, I have some news about what I found out about Mr. Gardeano."

"Great, let's eat first.," Colton replies with a smile as he sits at the table, and Gloria brings a plate of eggs and bacon with a side of toast. "Here you go, enjoy."

"No problem here. I have a feeling this is going to be a wonderful day."

When they finish eating, Gloria brings Colton a fresh cup of coffee and sits next to him.

"Okay, now listen to what I found out." As she picks up some pages from the table, she speaks, "I found some notes from when my husband was talking to his brother last year before he went on that last trip."

Colton is interested now. He leans forward on the table and says, "Okay, so tell me, what was it?'

Gloria continues, "Well, it seems that Mr. Gardeano is in the drug business. That was about a week before Charles went on that fateful flight."

Colton turned to Gloria and said, "okay, so tell me, what kind of drugs is it?"

Gloria continues, "All that Charles said in the notes was that he had found out that Mr. Gardeno was dealing in Fentanyl big time. It seems he was getting a steady supply in from Mexico every other month."

"No wonder he wanted to get George out of the gang. I wonder if George was aware of what Mr. Gardeano was doing? I think I'll ask George the next time I see him."

Gloria looks surprised at Colton, "Next time, did you see George when you went to see Mr. Gardeano? What was he doing with Mr. Gardeano?"

"Well, I only saw him for a moment at Mr. Gardeano's office."

"What did he say? Did he ask about me?" Gloria is getting excited, and Colton hears a little fear in her voice.

"Calm down, Gloria." Colton goes to Gloria, takes her by the arm, and turns her around, so she is facing him, and speaks, "Don't worry, I didn't tell him where you were."

"He knows now. I'm with you. He must have had those two men follow you last night. So, he knows I'm with you, oh, Colton, what are we going to do?"

"Don't worry, right after I finish this excellent breakfast you fixed. We are going to see my old friend, Jack Terrano. Remember, he is the Harbor Master here.

By early afternoon Colton and Gloria were walking up the steps to the office of the Harbor Master, Mr. Jack Terrano himself.

Jack is looking through the whole glass door and sees them approaching. He goes to the door and opens it, throws his hands up, and says, "Shit, it's my ole buddy Colton from across the water. How the hell are you?" They are both smiling and shaking hands like they were pumping the last water out of an old water pump.

Colton speaks first, "Jack, it is good to see you. What have you been up to these days? Leaving the women alone, I hope."

Jack laughs and says, "Only if I have to." Then looking at Gloria, he asks, "So, who's the pretty young lady you have there?"

"She is the reason we're here. Let me introduce you to Ms. Gloria Cambell, but she is a Widower and uses her given name now Gloria White. She is my client. Some men are after her, so she is staying on my boat for the time being."

Then Jack speaks, "Colton, I have somebody in the other room I want you to meet. You know her."

Jack goes into the other room and leaves Colton with a puzzled look on his face, turns, and shakes his shoulders at Gloria.

Jack comes back with this beautiful tall woman in tight jeans. Jack speaks, "Colton, I want you to meet,"

Just then, Colton turns and sees who it is, and a big smile comes over his face, and he says, "Margo Gibson, as I live and breathe, where in hell have you been all this time?"

Margo runs over to Colton, throws her arms around Colton, and says, "Colton, you old stick in the mud, where have you been. Gloria is looking uncomfortable and likes the third wheel. Colton turns and says to Gloria. "I want you to meet my old friend from Nam. Gloria, this woman, was the best martial artist in the company. I mean, she could have kicked anyone of us on our butts. I'm glad she was on our side."

Margo spoke, "Thanks Colton, but I wasn't that much of a badass."

Colton getting excited, now speaks, "Are you kidding? The three of us were together in the fall of Saigon in '75." remember that night we were in that bar in Ho Chi Minh City, and you took on those three guys from the 31st group when they were giving you a tough time." He looks at Margo and says, "Margo, I want you to meet my good friend Ms. Gloria White. She is in some trouble, and I'm trying to help her out. So, tell me, Margo, what have you been doing since you got back?"

Margo smiles and says, "Not much, picking up a job here and there, you know."

"What kind of job? What did you do after you left the Seals? I lost track of you."

"Well, I didn't go to college, so really I didn't have a skill set except what I learned in the Seals, so I did a lot of bodyguard work."

Colton smiles, snaps his finger, and speaks to Margo, "Say, why don't you work for me? You know I have a Private Eye agency. I could use someone like you to help, especially on this case."

Margo has a puzzled look on her face and speaks, "Well, what would I have to do?

Colton replies, "Do what you do best kick-ass and watch my back and my clients and your own and collect your paycheck. What do you say?

Margo looks at Jack and says, "What do you think, Jack?"

Jack shucks his shoulders then speaks, "Well, you would have money in your pocket. Hey, you know maybe you will like the work and eventually open your place P.I License and all. If you don't like it, you can always quit."

Margo thinks for minutes and says, "Yeah, your right. I'm pretty good at what I do." She turns to Colton and asks, "say do I carry a gun too?"

Colton speaks, "Well, not at first, but when you are ready, we could put in the paperwork for you to get one. What do you say?"

Margo smiles and says, "Yea, why not. When do I start?"

Colton continues talking, "Why don't we all go to dinner on me, and when we get back, I'll fill you and Jack in on my client's problem." Colton turns to Gloria and continues, "What do you say, Gloria? Is that all right with you?"

Gloria says with a smile, "Sure, why not? The more, the merrier."

CHAPTER ELEVEN

Well, that's the whole story, briefly, guys. Colton turns to Gloria and says, "Do you think we could get George, your husband's brother, to help us set a trap for Mr. Gardeano?"

Gloria looks at Colton and says, "It seems to me the night before Charles left on that faithful flight, he and George were having a pretty serious conversation about George helping his brother to bring Mr. Gardeano down."

"Great, did you happen to hear what it was?"

"No, I remember I wasn't feeling too well that night, and I went to bed early, and the next day, he was gone." Gloria started to cry but continued, "I usually kissed him good night, that night I didn't, and George took him to the Airport the next day. When I woke up, they were both gone."

Colton puts his arm around Gloria to console her and speaks, "That's okay, honey, don't worry about it. I'm sure he knew you wanted to. We'll ask George about his conversation with his brother when we see him."

Colton turns and looks at Jack and says, "Hey Jack do you mind if I borrow your car tomorrow to drive down to see Charles?"

Jack comes right back with, "Colton, I have a better idea, did you know that Margo has a car, she can drive you and her to see George? You are going to want Gloria here for safety reasons, right?" Colton is now getting excited. He turns to Margo and says, "How about it, Margo, like the good old days when we went on missions together?"

Margo replies, "I remember that you were walking ahead of me on that jungle mission, and you let that branch hit me in my face and busted my nose."

"Oh. Margo, you know that was an accident, and besides, I did say watch out, not my fault you were late in ducking."

"Yeah, right, I still owe you one for that." They both laughed, and Colton turned to Jack and said, "Jack, Gloria, and I can sleep aboard the boat tonight." Turning to Margo, he says, "Margo, how about we leave in the morning about nine after everyone eats breakfast?

Margo smiles and says, "Yeah, sure sounds good. Where do we have to go tomorrow?"

Before Colton could tell Margo where they were going, Jack jumped in with a smile, "you are having lunch at my house around 3:00 pm. All four of us." Everybody cheered as Colton took Margo and Gloria by the arm and led them to the front door. He said, "In the morning than people," as he walked the two women out the door.

On the way back to the boat, Colton explained his plan to Margo and Gloria.

"That's the plan briefly. What do you think, Margo?"

Margo shook her head, and with a smile on her face, she said, "Do you think that will work?"

Colton answers, "Well if the notes that Gloria found in her husband's papers are correct, I think George promised to finish his brother's job if Charles wasn't here. Well, it's late, and I think we should get some shuteye. We'll find out tomorrow.

CHAPTER TWELVE

They all met at Jacks' house for a late lunch the following day. They had just finished eating. Colton looks at his watch and speaks first, looking at Gloria, and says, "So now you are going to stay behind with Jack where I won't have to worry about you, right?"

"Yes, but I worry about you getting into trouble. You have George Campbell's address I gave you, right?"

Colton takes the piece of paper that Gloria gave him and reads it aloud, "7300 Lankershim Blvd. Apt. 1f." Looking at Gloria, and says, "Right."

Gloria says, "okay,"

Then turning and looking at Margo, Colton says, "Margo, pull your car around, and I'll meet you out front in a minute."

"Ok, Colton, don't be too long. It's four-thirty in the afternoon, and we have a way to go. If we are going to leave when you said." Margo goes outside. Colton turns to Jack and says, "Thanks for everything. Honey, I'll see you in the morning." keep an eye on my boat. It will be late when we get back, so I'll see you around noon tomorrow." Then he looks at Gloria and smiles

"You better, or I'll come to get you myself." Colton turns and leaves with a smile.

About two hours later, Margo pulled up in front of 7300 Lankershim Blvd. Colton and Margo get out of the, and Colton speaks first, "Margo, let me take the lead on this one, okay?"

Margo smiles at Colton, "Okay, Mr. Colton James, it is all yours. I'm just going watch your back."

They both get out of the car laughing. They walk over to the entrance of the building. They see the list of names on the buzzer plate. They look for Cambell and push the button. After a minute, a voice comes out of the voice box on the wall.

"Who is it, and what do you want?"

"Friend of Gloria, and we need to speak to you." They walk down the hall. After a minute, the door buzzer rings, and the door unlocks. Before they could reach door number 1F, it opens, and out steps, a middle-aged man with a beard dressed in dark pants and a sleeveless shirt speaks. "Yeah, what do you want?"

"Are you George Cambell, and your brother was Charles? Gloria spoke to me and asked me to help her with your boss Mr. Gardeano."

"I remember you, your, the guy that was in Mr. Gardeano's office last week asking about Gloria."

"Yep, that was me."

"Okay, come on in and have a seat. Who are you, and what can I do for you?"

"Thank you, mister, Cambell. I'm a friend of Gloria Cambell. My name is Colton James, and I'm a PI helping Gloria. We believe your boss Mr. Gardeano is dealing with drugs. More to the point, he is buying and selling Fentanyl. We would like you to help us find the stuff and turn it over to the cops."

"Oh, is that all? You must be crazy if you think I'm going to help you to do that."

"Mister Cambell, we believe your brother was trying to get you out of the gang that was connected to Mr. Gardeano when he found out about the drugs. But before he could get you free, unfortunately, flight ninety-three crashed.

Now, Mister Gardeano has tried twice to abduct your Sister-in-law to obtain what she knows about the drugs. I have her safe for the moment. We don't have much time left. What's it going to be, Mr. Cambell?"

Mr. Cambell starts walking around the room to figure out what he will do next. He turns and looks at Colton and speaks, "Mister James, I want to help, but if I tell you anything, Mister Gardeano will have me killed."

"Do you want out of the gang and not keep looking over your shoulder the rest of your life? Come with us right now and tell us what we need to know, and I'll promise to keep you safe. It is your choice, leave now and come with us..."

George looks at me, then at Margo, and says, "Ah, Hell. I don't need no stinking drugs; let's go."

Colton continues, "that sounds a line from an old movie, but I can't remember it at the moment."

Colton, Margo, and George made it back to Santa Barbara Harbor and Colton's Boat two hours later.

CHAPTER THIRTEEN

When they got back on board, 'THE WHO DONE IT,' Colton was surprised to see Gloria in the galley with some fresh coffee.

When she saw George coming through the door, she ran to him and hugged him and spoke, "Oh George, I was so worried about you."

George was a little uncomfortable with the attention she was giving him, "Oh hell, Glory, I'm fine, you don't have to worry. You know I can take care of myself."

"Yes, I know, but I still worry. Here sit; I'll get you some coffee. Gloria went over to the oven to pour him a cup of coffee and heard Colton speak, "Gloria, Margo, and I would love a cup too if you don't mind. I thought I was going to see you tomorrow at Jack's office."

"Oh sure, but I changed my mind, and Jack walked back here to the boat. Oh, Colton, I'm sorry. Go ahead and find a chair, all of you, and I'll bring the pot over to the table. I'm sorry, I was just glad to see George."

Colton continues, "Okay, George, why don't you tell me what Mr. Gardeano is up to with his drugs."

"Yeah, sure. Well, Mr. Gardeano is expecting a shipment to come at the end of this week."

Colon speaks, Let's see, that would be Saturday. So, we have four days to get ready. That will give us plenty of time to plan a surprise for him."

Margo jumps in, "What do you have in mind, Colton. Well, we don't know what time and exactly where he is going to be."

"Don't worry, George is going to get us all that information."

George speaks, "Me! I don't know the details. How am I going to tell you about them? He keeps that Information locked in his safe in the office. I don't know the combination to the safe that will open it."

Colton has a smile on his face when he speaks. "Margo, weren't you a safecracker in your other life?"

Now Margo looked surprised and said, "Well, yea, but that was before I joined the Marine Corp, and it was only a few jobs."

Colton speaks, "I heard the stories you used to tell in the Corp. They were all true, weren't they?"

Now Margo was red-faced, "Well, yes, they were all true but, that was a long time ago and, I have never gotten caught. I'm a little rusty now."

Colton continues, "Come on, Margo, it is like riding a bicycle, you don't forget, and with a little practice, you will be as good as new."

Margo heard herself say, "yes, I suppose your right. Let me check my books and see what I remember."

Colton, "All right, everyone, listen up. Margo, George, and I will make a little trip tomorrow night to Mr. Gardeano's office to see if we can find the safe in his office. George, do you know where in the office he keeps the safe?"

George replies, "Yes, behind the picture on the wall, right behind the chair at the desk. But I don't know the combination."

Colton jumps in, "That's okay, that's where Margo will look for the safe and go to work on it?

George, you stay in the car while Margo and I go in and see if we can find the journal with the information we need and take pictures with a camera on this phone. Just the pages that show the place and time they will pick up the drugs. When I'm finished taking the pictures, Margo and I will put the journal back in the exact position we found it, and we leave as quietly as we came. Any questions? Okay, then, let everyone go to bed if there are no questions. We have some big plans for the next couple of days."

CHAPTER FOURTEEN

The day had finally arrived. Margo is excited about the plan. The only concern she had was what brand of safe it would be. I told Margo, "George told me it was a Sentry."

Margo replied, "Oh, good, that's one of the easier ones to open."

The only concern I had was hoping everything would go off without a hitch. It was six p.m., and I went into the galley to get a cup of java. Margo was at the kitchen sink cleaning the last of the dishes.

"Say, Margo, what are you doing? It would help if you were resting. Are you all set for tonight?"

She turned and smiled at Colton and said, "I'm ready as I'm going to be. Are You?"

"Me? You have the hard part, not me."

"Yea, well, I'm doing fine. What time are we leaving?"

Colton looks at his watch, "Well, it's six pm. I figured we would leave the house at midnight. Not much traffic that time of the night, so it shouldn't take us long to get there."

Margo looked at Colton and asked, "Where is George?"

"Oh, George? He has been sleeping since after dinner. I figured I would wake him about ten pm."

Colton headed topside to go over his plan to make sure he had composed safely in his head and then decided to catch a nap.

Margo, meanwhile, was down at the galley reading over one of her books on safecracking. She felt good about herself and thought, 'well, I remember more than I thought I did; I'm ready.'

It was a little bit past 10:00 pm when Margo woke up checked her watch. She closed the book and looked at the clock in the galley; it said 07:00 pm. Margo decided to catch a nap. Then she went to find Colton.

She found Colton sleeping in one of the deck chairs. She went over and woke him, saying, "Say, Colton, it is time to wake George; it's 10:30 pm."

Colton jumped up, being startled by Margo. He wiped his face with both hands and looked at Margo. "Okay, Margo, see that George is awake and put the things we need to take in the car. I'm going to wash my face to wake me a little. I'll meet you in the car in ten minutes, okay?"

Margo, "Gotcha, Colton, see you in ten. We will be ready."

CHAPTER FIFTEEN

They made suitable time getting back to North Hollywood. It is only one-thirty a.m. They parked about a block from Mr. Gardeano's office. All three get out of the car, and George speaks first. "Say, Colton, what do you want me to do?"

Colton speaks in a deep voice point to an alley between the two buildings. At the end of the backstreet, there is a door. "George, that door looks like the back entrance to the Office of Mister Gardeano. So, you give us a couple of minutes, then go straight up the street over there. When you get to the corner, cross Lankershim to the other side and hide in the doorways of one of the stores. If you see anything suspicious call me on my cell phone. We shouldn't be any more than fifteen minutes. Got it?"

"Gotcha, chief. Good luck with finding the Journal."

Colton and Margo head across the street and down the alley to the back door. After a minute or two, the door opens, and George takes off down the Alley. When George gets to Lankershim Blvd, he crosses to the other side of the street and to the front entrance of a sports store, which is hidden indirectly from the boulevard. George has a perfect view in both directions of Lankershim. The best is that he can see the front door to Mr. Gardeano's office right across the street from where he is standing.

By now, Colton and Margo have managed to open the back door and shut off the alarm before it could go off.

Margo speaks first, "Okay, Colton, where did George say the safe was?"

Colton points behind the desk and says, "He said, it is behind the office desk behind the picture hanging on the wall. Pointing to the picture on the wall behind the desk. Over there."

Margo speaks, "Colton, you were right. Margo takes the picture from the wall, and sure enough, there is a safe in the wall. The safe is a Sentry; it looks like a new one too."

George replies, "Yeah, but can you open it?"

Margo, "Hell, yeah."

Just then, Colton's cell phone rings. Colton signals Margo SH as he answers. He listens, a minute and then hangs up. He Walks over to Margo and whispers, "Margo, quiet until I tell you everything is okay. George just called to say a security guard; checks the front doors to make sure they are locked. George said he'll call us when the guard is gone past the door and down the street." Margo gives him the okay sign.   Colton's phone rings again a few minutes later, and Colton answers. After a minute, he hangs up and tells Margo to go ahead and open the safe while Colton waits.

After a few minutes, Colton hears a click on the safe door and asks Margo, "Did you get it?"

Margo replied, "Of course, what do you think I came along for?"

Colton speaks, "I was beginning to wonder." Colton walks to the safe where Margo is standing. "Step aside. I got it from here, Margo." Colton reaches in the safe for a couple of books on the second shelf and reads the titles. The top one says on the outside cover 'scheduled incoming shipments.' He puts the second book on the top shelf, takes the top one, and opens it on the desk. He starts checking pages. After he turns a few pages, he comes to

Saturday's schedule. He leaves the book open, takes out the cell phone, and takes pictures of the pages. When He gets to the last page, he speaks, "Well, the last page. Now let's put it back exactly where it was, close the safe, and get the hell out of here. Margo, give a check and make sure nothing is out of place. While I call George and let him know we are finished and, on our way out."

Margo says, "Sure, Colton, I got this. Go ahead and make the call."

On the way out the door, Colton stop, turns, and says to Margo, "Hey kiddo, make sure you put the alarm back on, turn out all the lights and make sure this door is locked."

Margo replies to Colton, "I'm right behind you. See you outside."

By the time Colton and Margo get to the corner of Lankershim Boulevard, George is there with the car. George slides over to the front right side, passenger seat. He remembers this as Margo's car she is driving. So, he climbs out, gets in the back, and shuts the door. Colton slides over to the right side of the front seat. Margo is the last one to climb in behind the wheel and, off down the street, they went.

It was about 3:30 am and, there were no cars on the road. I thought to myself, 'by the way, Margo drives, we will be in Santa Barbara in an hour. I'll take a nap.'

They made suitable time driving back to the Santa Barbara Marina. The whole bunch was worn-out, and they all found their respective bunks and called it a night. Colton put his camera with the journal under his pillow, not wanting to lose it even by mistake.

They all slept late except for Colton; he wanted to read the journal alone to grasp it all without being interrupted. After reading it a few times, he decided to see the Harbor Master Jack Terrana ask his opinion. He left a note on the table telling Margo and George where he was going so they wouldn't wonder when they woke up.

Colton was approaching the building that housed Jack's office and went in. Then headed up to the second floor to his office and knocked on the door.

Jack opens the door, sees Colton, and says, "Back so soon? Well, did you have a successful trip?"

Colton walks in the door with a happy look on his face and says, "Sure did. We got home around 2:00 am. We all went to bed except me. I stayed up and read the journal from the schedule."

Jack smiled and said, "Well, come on over and sit down and tell me all about it while I'll fix you some coffee."

Colton is serious, "Jack, I have a question about the Schedule instructions."

Jack speaks, "Okay, hit me up for it. I'm ready."

Colton starts to speak, "As far as Jurisdiction goes, who has it west of Catalina Island about five miles." I have the longitude and latitude on the instructions here." He hands the pages from the journal to Jack to read and waits for his reaction. He didn't take long. "Jack, where did you get this information?"

Colton puts his hand over his heart and proudly says, "I cannot tell a Lie. I plead the fifth."

Jack jumps in with, "I take it you got it illegally from somebody's desk and, he doesn't, know you got it. Right?

Colton comes right back with, "Trust me; you are better off not knowing. Just tell who we can give it to that you found it in the trash can in North Hollywood.

Jack, "Is this for real?"

"Okay, Jack, who can you trust to give it to?"

Jack moves around his office for a minute, trying to think who he could contact for help?"

Finally, Jack stops at the window and turns and speaks, "I know somebody I can trust, but you have to explain the pages to him. I'll give him a call this afternoon and see if he can come over to my office tonight. Make sure you are here at 8:00 pm." He hands the journal pictures back to Colton. I'll be back at eight sharp.

CHAPTER SEVENTEEN

Eight sharp, Colton knocks on Jack Terrano's office door. After a minute or so, Jack opens the door, smiles, and says, "Colton, comes on in the office. I want you to meet someone." Colton comes in and sees a gentleman in uniform. Colton walks over to the desk and sits in one of the chairs.

"Jack continues to speak, "I want you to meet Commander Garrod; he is stationed at the local Coast Guard station here. I was hoping you could tell him exactly what you told me."

Colton says, "okay. First Commander, can I ask you if you have ever heard the name Albert Guardeano in your travels?"

The Commander looks at both men and then says, "I believe I have; Isn't he the one that does a lot of drug trafficking between Los Angeles and the Mexican border?"

Colton speaks first, "As a matter of fact, he is the same person. Commander, I'm a private investigator. At this particular time, I'm trying to help a woman whose husband until he died in a well-known plane crash on 9/11. It was flight ninety-three. After his death, his wife came to me for some help. Mister Gardeano was threatening her. It seems that her husband Charles Cambell was trying to get his brother out of the gang Mister Gardeano headed back in Pa. when he was just a second-rate gangster. George, Charles's brother, was in the club, and his brother was trying to get him out, and Mister Gardeano was giving him a tough time. So, he asked his brother to help him, and a little time went by, and Charles was killed in that plane crash and Misses Cambell changed her name back to her given name and moved out here to hide from him. Now she is Ms. White. Anyway, let's get to where I could help you. I have proof so you can Capture Mr. Gardeano for Drug Trafficking. I have some reliable information that could convict Mister Gardeano, and you could put him away for good. What do you say?"

The Commander rises and speaks. "Well, first, I would have to ask you where you got this information?"

Colton stands and looks at the Commander and then at Jack. Jack looks back at Colton and shrugs his shoulders. Colton looks back at the Commander and says, "Would you believe me if I said I found it?"

Commander smiles and says, "We find a lot of things here in California. I'll tell you what you give me the information now, and we'll decide later as to where it was found?"

Colton is relieved, smiles, and then tells the Commander, "Sir, you are a man with a plan. I like that. He then hands the pictures of the pages to the Commander and tells him, "There is a shipment coming in at those longitudes. It is all yours. And I'll wait to hear from you."

The Commander speaks, "You better be right, Mister James, or it is going to be you who will be in a lot of trouble. Good Day, sirs."

He goes to the door and leaves. When the door shuts, Jack looks at Colton and says, "I hope you are right about all this, Colton."

Colton looks at Jack and says, "Oh, I'm right, all right. I hope it doesn't go sideways. Well, we will know come tomorrow night. Myself, George, Margo, and Gloria will be on my boat until we hear from the Commander tomorrow night. See Ya."

CHAPTER EIGHTEEN

Sunday at Two p.m.

Colton is standing at Jack Terrano's office entrance, looking at his watch. Thinking to himself. 'Now is the time for good men like me to find out what happened.' And shakes his head, and then he knocks twice, and he hears Jack says, "Come on in, old buddy, the Commander isn't here yet, you are either early, or he is late."

Colton opens the door and walks in. Jack points to the chair and says. "Colton, sit. The commander should be here at any minute."

Colton replies, "I didn't sleep much last night; I kept thinking about the Commander, saying I might be the one who might be in trouble."

Jack laughs and says, "No, relax, Colton, everything went as planned. I'll let the Commander tell you. Don't worry, and it was all good."

Colton takes a deep breath and says, "Ah, well, that's a relief."

They both hear someone knock on the door, and Jack says, "Come on in, Commander, we were all here awaiting the news of your little adventure last night."

The Commander walks over to Colton, holds his hand, and says, "Mister James, first let me tell you, your information was spot on, and we comprehended all those involved with the drugs. There were two boats involved, and we got both of them. We haven't counted all the drugs yet. But I can tell you we broke the ring for this area, thanks to you. You will be getting a commendation for your help in this matter."

Colton got one of those sly smiles on his face and spoke, "Thank Commander, I was glad to be of help, was anybody hurt?"

"Well, Colton, now that you mentioned it, we had one fatally, the Leader of the whole thing, Mr. Gardeano, was shot in the head, and we recovered the body. The rest of them will be going to jail for a long time."

Colton wanted to get out of there and get back and tell Gloria and George the good news. He stands up and says to both men, "Well, I guess I can go now. My work is finished. Jack, thanks for everything, and it was seeing you. I'm sure I'll be seeing you again. He turns to the Commander, shakes his hand, and says, "Commander, I can't thank you enough for the help. It was a pleasure collaborating with you."

Before Colton could get to the door, the Commander turned and spoke, "Oh Colton, I'll walk you to your car, do you mind?."

Colton replies, "No, of course not. I'll wait outside." He turns and shuts the door as he leaves and waits outside.

After a few moments, the Commander walks out, shuts the door, and looks at Colton. And the Commander speaks. "Colton, I just wanted to tell you we found the Journal in Mr. Gardeano's safe when we searched his office. You did an excellent job. We have to keep our Informants undercover, you know." He smiles and Winks, and then he heads toward his boat.

EPILOGUE

When Colton returned to 'The Who Done It." He found everybody sitting in the galley chatting and laughing and drinking coffee around the table.

He walks into the galley and speaks, "Well, I'm glad everybody is here. I have something important to say; first, Gloria, honey, could you get me a cup of coffee?"

Sure honey, have a seat, and I'll bring you a cup. Everybody is waiting to hear what happened. Gloria comes back with the coffee, gives it to Colton, and sits and says, okay, now tell us the results of our little trip to Mr. Gardeano's

"Okay then, I spoke to Commander Garrod, and he said that everything came off without a hitch. Let me say one thing about Mr. Gardeano: he is dead. He was the only one that died. He was shot in the head trying to escape." Colton looked at Gloria, and she had what only could be called a relief look on her face; she looked over at George and smiled.

Colton continued, "Mr. Gardeano's whole gang was apprehended along with all the drugs. The best news is nobody has to appear in front of the judge. "I'm happy to say this case is closed, also everybody can go home anytime they want to.

Colton continues, "Well, I don't know about you guys, but I'm going to bed. It's been a long day, so, goodnight, everybody." Colton turns and heads to his stateroom.

The smell of fresh coffee awakens Colton. Thinking it's the morning, he rises from his bed. He notices it is still dark outside. Colton looks at his clock on the dresser; it says, one forty-five in the morning. Now he thinks somebody left the coffee and was burning it. That's when he realizes that Gloria hasn't come to bed. So, Colton gets up, puts his pants on, and goes to the galley. There is no one there when he arrives but a pot of coffee brewing. He goes over and pours himself a cup, turns the coffee off, and goes topside to see if Gloria is there.

When he reaches the deck, he looks around for Gloria, and he sees her leaning on the boat's rail at the stern part of the boat. He walks up to her and speaks.

"Gloria, honey, couldn't sleep?"

She is startled, turns quickly, sees Colton, and says, "Oh, it is you. Yeah, I couldn't sleep, so I came up here to do some thinking."

Colton steps closer and speaks, "About…What?"

Gloria looks at Colton for a minute without saying and looks into his eyes and speaks, "We not that the case over. I have to go home."

Colton, looking a little surprised but inside, knew he didn't love her enough to ask her to stay.

Colton looks at her and says, "Well, I can drive you and George back to your hotel, and you can take care of everything from there."

Gloria looks back at Colton and says, "Okay, let me wake George. We will be ready to go in a bit.

The End